The Golden Aspen

by

Cheryl A. Price

AuthorHouse™
1663 Liberty Drive
Bloomington, IN 47403
www.authorhouse.com
Phone: 1-800-839-8640

First published by AuthorHouse 8/24/2009

ISBN: 978-1-4389-6101-9 (sc)

Library of Congress Control Number: 2009908356

Printed in the United States of America
Bloomington, Indiana

This book is printed on acid-free paper.

For My Mom

Many years ago, in the mountains of what we now know as Colorado, there lived a small tree. The young tree stood only three feet tall and was so small that the cedars and cottonwoods towered above it.

The taller trees looked down on the tree, because it did not have the strength of the scrub oak that lived nearby. It did not have the beautiful blue-green needles of the fir trees that grew in abundance on the steep slopes that stretched up the mountains. Nor did it have the color of the yellow-green needles of the ponderosa pine that dotted the mountains. It had no friends nearby and its closest relatives were the willows that bent and swayed in a valley far to the east.

The columbine and sunflower plants splashed their color at the roots of some of these trees and the hoods of the blue lupine spread among the plants of the plains that led up to the mountains. The little tree loved to peek through the shrubs and bushes that surrounded it and the other trees. When it looked toward the plains far away, it saw long green grasses, clover and yellow poppies, and red paintbrush flowers that enveloped the meadows in the distance. In the winter, when the wildflowers disappeared, it saw cactus burst forth with red flowers that crowned their thorny heads.

The tree was thin, with small green leaves and white bark. At the slightest breeze it would tremble, while the other trees stood bold and straight in spring, summer, fall and winter.

"Look how that small tree shakes in the breeze," said the cedar.

"It isn't worthy to be called a tree," sniffed the fir as it looked down on the little tree. "I will call it an aspen."

"Yes, a quaking aspen," the fir laughed.

The tree grew rapidly, but it could never keep up with its larger neighbors. The shrubs and grass in this mountain region at times engulfed the little tree, which became known by the name Aspen.

The animals that lived in the area noticed the tree's small, heart-shaped leaves. The rabbit, raccoon, and marmots would gather round the tree and deer and elk often visited the young tree. But neither the elk nor deer ever ate the leaves or the soft white bark of the young tree. When these larger animals stopped by the small tree, they would nuzzle it and tell it not to be afraid of being so small.

"Someday you will grow up and the other trees will look to you as one of the finest trees on the mountain," a young stag told it.

"Someday you will grow strong and hardy," a snowy white owl told the tree.

"I know you are wise," the young tree said. "But when will that be?"

"I do not know when," the owl said. "I have seen many trees in this forest, but none like you. These other trees which look down upon you now will someday hail you as a prince of the forest."

When the fir and cedar trees heard this from the owl, they looked down upon the small tree and laughed.

"You will never be more than a puny tree," the scrub oak told the little tree.

"No more than a puny tree," the cedar repeated.

"Pay no heed to those trees," said the gray wolf, which stopped under the tree to look over the meadow far away. "We love you. You are the best of trees."

The seasons went by and the aspen grew to ten feet in height. But even though it had grown taller, it still had no friends among the trees close by. So it looked to the animals and birds that roamed the mountainside for companionship. It loved the butterflies, which flew down to the wildflowers and the plains, and asked them to tell him about the marvelous flowers they saw from a distance. It asked the owl about the eagles it saw on the rocky red cliffs of the mountain.

"The eagle flies great distances," said the owl. "I dare not come close to it, and the other animals fear it."

The gray wolf had grown older and one day told the aspen of some of its journeys. "There is a great river that runs through the mountains. It makes the roar of thunder as it crashes down the valleys it rushes through. I have also seen strange animals that walk on two legs."

"A great stream? Animals that walk on two legs?" the young tree repeated.

"What the gray wolf says is true," said the snowy owl. "I have seen these strange creatures too. The creatures that walk on two legs are called people."

The little tree listened to their words and wondered at what they described.

One day as it looked over the meadowland far to the east, the tree saw something approaching the mountains.

That must be what the owl and the wolf spoke about two seasons past, the tree decided.

The little aspen called out to the owl, "Who approaches from where the wildflowers grow?"

The owl opened wide its gold colored eyes and scanned the fields and meadows beneath the mountain's slope.

"I see what you see," the owl said. "I believe it is one of those creatures of which the gray wolf and I spoke. I will spread my wings and fly toward it and come back and tell you what it is."

The owl flew from its perch on a branch of an oak tree and was carried by the wind toward the meadows beneath. The aspen watched as it circled over the meadows high above the creature and then came back to the mountain slope to report its findings.

"It is one of those creatures that walk on two legs," the owl said. "I spent some time close to where these creatures live when I was young. The older creatures are called 'men' and 'women.' The one that approaches is young. However, he is not like those I saw to the south or even among our valleys and mountains. He walks with a long staff, taller than he is. His skin is burned by the sun. I think what he is wearing is called a 'robe,' and it covers him from his head to his knees. He walks as if he carries a great burden, but I see nothing on his shoulders."

The tiny tree grew curious. "Is he coming this way?"

"I think he is," the owl responded.

The tree waited and wondered if he would ever see what the wise old owl had seen. Two days later the boy approached, and the tiny tree welcomed his arrival.

"You have come far," the aspen said. "Rest beneath my branches and I will shelter you when night approaches."

The boy with the long staff understood what the tree said. He thanked the tree and sat down beneath its narrow trunk and thin branches. Although its leaves were beginning to shake with the approach of the evening breeze, the little tree spread its branches over the stranger. The night became cold and an early snow threatened the young boy, whose thin clothing provided little warmth.

"I am afraid for you," the little tree said. "You are shivering from the cold. Let me call my friends to protect you. Sometimes great winds come through the mountains. They can do much harm to the unwary."

Through chattering teeth, the boy agreed.

The young tree called out to its friends—the stag, the marmot, the wolf, the rabbits, the mighty elk, and a small black bear to help the stranger. The animals all came and gathered round the tree and the stranger. They saw how the cold was affecting the boy, and for the sake of their friend, the aspen, they lay down near the boy and used their own bodies to keep him warm.

By morning the cold wind was gone and the animals arose and went their way. The young boy said to the tree, "You sheltered me from the storm. I will not forget your kindness."

"You must go?" the tree asked.

"Yes. I have much to do. But someday I will return."

The young tree watched as the boy grasped his staff and walked back toward the east from where he had come.

Fifteen seasons came and went. The owl and the wolf had grown old with age. Other animals came and often visited the tree, which stood thirty-five feet in height. Despite its growth, it still was not accepted by the other trees on the mountain. That did not matter anymore to the tiny tree. It had many friends among the animals, birds, and butterflies it saw each year. It now liked to gaze on the wildflowers it saw on the distant meadow.

One day, as the aspen stretched beneath the sunny sky, its leaves slightly stirring in the warm sun, the snow-white owl looked to the east and saw a man approaching.

"I see someone," the owl screeched.

"I see someone," said the gray wolf.

The rabbits and marmots gathered round to see who approached.

The man came closer. He was dressed in a white robe and held a shepherd's staff in one hand. The young tree thought he saw a red scar on the man's forehead. The animals scurried to watch the man from a distance as the stranger approached the young aspen.

"Long ago you sheltered me from a storm in these mountains," the stranger told the tree.

"You were smaller then, but you called your friends here to help and protect me. I told you I would return, and I have."

The owl nodded its head and whispered to the marmot, "I think the moment has come that I foresaw for our young friend."

"Yes, wise owl. The moment has come," the man said. He turned to the tree. "Because you sheltered me and called others to help me, I will mark that moment in your life. In the fall of the year, when winter approaches, your leaves will turn golden in color. Your descendents will share this mark of favor. You will be called the 'king of the mountain forest,' because you will wear the gold of royalty."

The tree, which was not so tiny anymore, bent forward. "I do not know what to say," he said.

The man smiled. "You do not need to say anything. Your actions were enough."

Then, as the animals, birds, and flowers celebrated the honor bestowed on their friend, the stranger vanished.

The tree grew and as the man promised, it had many descendents. Each year the trees that bear the mark the stranger placed upon them glow a glorious gold. Today, the descendents of that once tiny tree crown the mountains with shimmering gold.

THE END

Cheryl A. Price has written for newspapers and journals. She is a former librarian and newspaper editor. A biography, written by Ms. Price, was published in 2004. It tells the life story of Thomas L. Thomas, from his years in an orphanage to his experiences as a prisoner of war during World War II. It has been purchased throughout the United States and abroad and has been read and reread by troops serving in Iraq. The Golden Aspen is inspired by the beauty of the Aspens of Colorado and is the author's first children's book. She holds three masters' degrees in history, library science and communications.

LaVergne, TN USA
01 September 2009
156615LV00003B

9 781438 961019